Rush

Of

Many

Waters

Also by Pauly Hart

Rush of Many Waters:

Volume Two

By Pauly Hart

Contents

Shorts

Day Faith

At the end of the day as I was walking home, I found a man lying on the ground who had been beaten. His shirt was torn, and his face was bloody and crying. He was pleading with me with big watery eyes, but I was running a little late for my favorite show. I came to my house. The neighbor's cat had been sick, and had left a lovely present for me on my doorstep... I almost avoided stepping in it. As I walked in and threw my keys on the counter, the wall-phone beeped. I kicked my shoes into the corner. Wasn't going to wear them again anyway.

It was Denise. She had been in Detroit for the last couple of days on business, and had decided to give me a ring because she felt obligated. Her call was meaningless. I half-listened to her as she rampaged against the politics of major car corporations - and hung up the phone when I couldn't take it anymore. Immediately she called back, but I just watched the phone as it rang, trying to imagine her frustration on the other end of the line. Eventually she must have gotten tired with the whole ordeal, because the phone quit ringing. I watched it for a good ten minutes before I eventually decided just to cut the cord on the line. Snip. Try to call me now.

I decided it was time to eat. Going to the freezer, I realized that I had bought nothing in the past month that even closely resembled sustenance. I ate anyway. Frozen biscuits usually taste better cooked... I didn't mind. I plopped into my chair, just in time to catch the credits of my show. Damn Denise. Damn her to Hell.

Oh well... I stood up and kicked the TV in. Another day. Deciding whether to sleep in my suit or pajamas took up the better part of the next hour. I eventually determined that my suit just didn't feel good anymore... I stripped it off in the living room and pushed it into the corner. Much better.

I studied myself in the bathroom mirror. The same tired shoulders, the same haggard face, the same graying hair. I staggered to the bedroom, I coughed up blood and phlegm into my hand, and wiped it on the wall before I collapsed onto the bed with the grace of a corpse. I lay there, and laid there. All my life seemed to be wrapped up in today.

I had gone to the doctor again today and he told me that my condition had not improved. As a matter of fact, it had grown worse. Much worse. If I sleep, I die. I haven't slept in fifteen years. I lay in bed and do not sleep. There are exactly twenty-two thousand, three hundred and thirty-seven dots on my ceiling. I finished counting them again last night.

I'm done counting my dots.

I'm done counting on my luck.

Goodnight. I'm going to sleep.

An Island at the End of Time

1

"Hello." He said, the dark wind whipping his black cloak behind him as the rough sea sprayed foam on her dress.

"Hello." She said in return.

The sky was red, as it always was. The days had been growing darker and darker stars had fallen from the sky. It was the last few days of earth and everyone knew it.

She had responded to his post on Craigslist. The world, as they both had known it, had not collapsed as it did in most movies. The power was still on and things had progressed as they normally did when the world was not ending. People had gone to work. People had gone to church. They had done things as they always had before the announcement.

It was almost surreal.

He had expected things to fall into ruin quickly but even he had gone to work as normal. He was just like everyone else it seemed. Except for the cosplay.

Well not really cosplay. Not in the sense that he was living out a Japanese animation. But he did have on a chainmail hauberk and a lion's helm underneath his upholstery fabric cloak. There he was standing next to the sea, next to a maiden in a jade green satin dress.

"Do you do this often?" He asked her, laughing.

"No, there's a first time for everything." She responded, almost sighing.

"Oh." he said. "I guess the stars really changed everything."

"Yes. Something like that." She said. "Here, take my hand. Let's walk for a while."

He took her hand in his, a small delicate thing. He looked at her face. He had not really understood that it was beautiful when he had first seen her online, but now, from a profile, he noticed. She was very lovely indeed. Her small features reminded him of a sunset, pleasing to place your eyes on.

"Watch out for the rocks." She cautioned him as he almost tripped on one and fell into the sea. He had nearly escaped placing his foot on a very unstable rock. This part of the beach was mostly sand, but there were large and small outcroppings of black metamorphic rock here and there. In the distance, a pheasant called.

The volcanic island had been active in the sense that only geologists say. The last eruption had been over 400 years ago. It was just another island in the middle of the Pacific Ocean. The only inhabitant here was him and now her, and the pilot – who was scheduled to leave after refueling.

The island that was now his had been something of a fluke to own. A Sheikh of an affluent Arab country had sold it to him for one dollar. The Sheikh had flown him out to the island and given him a tour, then the keys and codes and then left him there, taking all of the employees with him, to Medina. That was a month ago…

The fact that the world was ending had everything to do with the ownership of the island and his immediate wealth. It had been a nice change, but lonely. When the big announcement had been made about the imminent death the world four years ago, life had … Well…

It didn't matter. What mattered now was the girl.

"What is your name at least?" He asked her for the first time in real life.

"I've told you all that you need to know. The main thing you need to remember is that I have agreed to come here and by you."

"Well, and the fact that you had… how did you put it… 'Nothing else really going on'?"

She laughed. It was a bell. Delicate, like her hands.

"Sure," he said. Resigning himself to her ways.

The walk was the same one he took every day. Around the beach, then stopping by the river and back. The north part of the island was the only part that had any beach at all. It was here that there was a stream that met the ocean. It was dammed and controlled and the main water processing plant was directly on top of the artesian opening, but from here, it looked raw and natural.

There had been steps built in to the mountainside that led up the way into the plateau that was under the house. The house faced north as well, and the view to the sea was uninhibited. From the house, looking down, you could see the gardens directly below them, the airstrip and maintenance hangar to the east and the pier and docks to the west. Behind the house, to the south, was the small island road that made a circular route around the back.

The Sheikh had been generous and kind to him. He had left several jet skis, a medium sized fishing boat and a small Jeep. Though it would not matter, there was also food and provisions enough to last another twenty years.

The complex, which was the house, and several out-buildings, ran entirely on solar power. God knows there was enough sunshine here to power a thousand more homes just like this one.

But nothing else mattered besides the house now, the woman now, and the death just a few days away.

2

They ate a light lunch. Salmon and quiche with a spinach and dandelion salad. She said it was fine and then they changed into bathing suits. The garden had a full sized pool, and she said that she would like to swim a little before the evening. Which was fine. He could use a dip too.

"No." She said. "I would like to swim alone, if you do not mind."

He said that he didn't mind and that he would await her in the living room. She agreed.

The living room was a great room that adjoined the entire house together. The ceiling could be removed if you wanted to let in the outdoor weather. In the middle of the room was a large Melaleuca tree that had its first branches above the roof-line. The left and right partitions of the roof would close together around the tree. A large rubber collar enclosed the tree, half-circle on each side of the partition. The Sheikh had a tap installed on the tree that gathered the essential oils, and had lectured him on its proper usage for over an hour. He had never tried to get any oil from the tree... What was the point of living longer when they were all going to die?

The library was stocked with a great selection of American PBS shows. The complete 1979 - 1989 This Old House, Nova, POV and many others. He had asked the Sheikhh about the This Old House collection. "Bob Villa or nothing!" was the Sheikh's angry reply. Currently in the laserdisc was Washington Week in Review, Week one and two, August 1978. He had become immediately addicted to the show and watched it as much as he could. Paul Duke had been a better change than Robert MacNeil, but he was no Max Kampelman. The laserdisc set had been massive. Everything from 1980 on was on Blu-ray and you could hold five episodes per disc, not two. He had heard the airplane take off when she was swimming. He should probably check to see if the pilot had turned off the avgas pump. It was the only responsible thing to do anyway. What fun would the island be if it was on fire?

He walked out the side garden path on his way down to the airstrip. "I'm going out to check the airstrip!" he called out to her.

"Alright!" She called back.

It wasn't far, maybe a quarter of a mile down the path. She hadn't brought much with her when she had arrived. The pilot had dropped the bags off on the little trolley and asked where to pump up. He didn't want to stay for food. This was only a favor for a friend. His last trip, the pilot had said. Now he was gone.

When she had arrived almost two hours ago, there had been no words. Only the moving of the bags and the walk down to the beach and the small conversation in between. The pilot had indeed put up the pump and locked it down and placed the key back where it belonged. There was no need really for security on the island. You would be able to hear a plane landing and the security fence was very high and electrified at the top, so nothing other than the pheasants could get over.

Pheasants. Brown and blue and bright red and gold. They were everywhere and they always seemed to make plenty of noise. They were beautiful but they never shut up. He had trapped and eaten several of them during my first few weeks here, so now they stayed away from the compound. He didn't mind the other birds, the Lyrebirds. They were hilarious and sometimes he would stay out with them, teaching them new songs to impress their ladies. They didn't get too close to the house during the daytime, but at night, would shelter up on the roof coop. Their only predator was the other import to the island by the Sheikh, the Margay.

Margays are the smallest species of cat on the planet. Populating most of South America, they are one of the only (if not the only) species of New World Cat to live only in trees and not come down to the ground. They are also capable of mimicking the voices of other animals. Often at night, they call. Some nights he thinks that the Lyrebirds have gotten out, only to see the reflective eyes in the trees of the cats hunting them with their own song. They are the only reason that he locks the doors.

3

She is done with her swim when he returns to the house. She is waiting in the living room, hair wrapped in a towel, nothing else on. "I was thinking of doing this now, to see if it works." She said. "If we do not like it, we do not have to do it again. If we do like it, we will be happy we did not wait long." The wraparound white leather couch complimented her still damp skin perfectly. She lay down on the seat, draped her left leg over the back-rest and her right leg on the floor. Looking at him sideways she asked: "Well? What do you think?"

He thought it was just fine. Every bit of her was shaved and pretty. She smelled like sun-drenched tangerines and when he entered her, it was heavenly.

Thirty minutes later, she allowed him to kiss her tenderly on the cheek. They showered together in the rain room and then he made them supper. Penne with chicken and broccoli in a light alfredo sauce. Applesauce cake for dessert. Then more lovemaking. This time however, she was not so casual. She led him by the hand into the master bedroom and they took their time. Whipped cream and strawberries. Plenty of kissing. Mouth, hands, legs, everywhere. It was sunset when they were done. She sighed and told him that she was glad she had responded to the ad.

He had run the ad in every craigslist in North America. She had responded from the Omaha, Nebraska site and they had begun their conversation. It had been nervous at first, but the more he told her about the place, the more she had fallen in love with it. "Newerwoman5" was the name she had given herself in the conversations. They had one VOIP face-to-face phone call and they had sealed the deal then. The only thing left was to fly her out.

He got up from the bed, thought about showering again, but, as it was late, he showed her how to lock down the house.

"But what do we have any fear from?" She had asked him.

"The cats." was all he had said, as he showed her each door.

After the stars had fallen, things had become really strange. There had been public announcements about this leader and that leader... It didn't really matter, out here on the island... At least the sea wasn't red any more, that was a relief.

"Here and here." He clicked the locks down with the electronic keypad. The interface was like a small computer, located in the hallway just before the living room. The living room ceiling and adjoining doors clicked and buzzed with an audible *clack* that was very reassuring. You could get to the kitchen around the living room by the adjoining hallway, but he always locked everything anyway. It just felt safer.

"The cats... They only hunt at night?" She asked.

"Well yes." He said. "And they only hunt the birds."

"That's relieving." She said. "So, why lock the doors at all?" She asked, hand on his arm.

"Just a precaution." He said. Inside he wondered if it was more than that.

4

The next morning, they ate again - A simple breakfast of figs and cereals. He wants to show her the island. They dress medieval again. She has the perfect dress complete with a hennin (the "dunce cap" hat). It is sky blue and has long sheaves of blue ribbon down the sides. He loves it and tells her so.

"Glad you think so." She said, and takes his arm as they walk out to the garage to get the Jeep.

"Would you like to see where the lyrebirds sleep?"

"Well yes. I suppose I would." She replied.

It is on the roof of the garage where the Sheikh kept the lyrebird cages. Row after row of perfect coops. Designed to where the birds could get in but the margays could not. The only drawback was that he had to let them out every morning.

There is blood and feathers everywhere by the outside steps to the coops. Her foot scrapes the gravel.

"Dear Jesus!" she says. Is it like this every morning?"

"Good god, no. The cats must have gotten in over the fence." He grips her arm. "Stay here." he says and walks up the steps to the roof.

"Holy shit!" He exclaims and she is on the roof in seconds behind him. Every cage is ripped open and mangled bodies are everywhere. Blood and grizzle are on the ground in buckets. Here, there was a severed Lyrebird, snapped in two. In another spot, an entire wing, ripped savagely out of the body. It was a complete massacre. There was not a spot on the roof where there was not blood. She vomited.

At the sound of her convulsions, they heard a wet mewing. In the far corner of the rooftop a margay lay, dying. Its low dark mew was sickening and when it did not mew, it wheezed.

"Stay here," he said.

"Not a chance." she said, gripping his arm harder than before.

Although it seemed a bit foolish, he did have a dagger on his belt. It was just for show, mind you, but it would do the trick. He pulled it out and held it in his left hand while they gingerly walked around most of the mess to the cat. When he was three feet away, he stomped the ground and yelled "HA!" to see if he could get any response from the cat. Nothing.

The dying animal wheezed and mewed again.

"Reeeeeeeoooooooooo" it said, quietly. How had it died? From the side it looked unharmed, which is why he thought maybe it was just playing at being dead.

Now, for all intents and purposes, a margay looks exactly like a Jaguar's kitten. A miniature version of the larger cat. They circled around the other side of the cat and he nudged it with his boot. Nothing. Then he rolled it over. Blood everywhere, but where was the wound?

There was no wound. Quick, like a housecat on a hardwood floor, the Margay scrambled up on all fours, dancing on the tile. Rising on its legs, arching *moans* and *meowls* erupted above them in the Melaleuca tree that towered above their head. Their hearts were in their mouths as they slowly looked up to behold the tree above them, full of all the margays from all over the island. There must have been a hundred. They had come in all around him as they were focused on the body below. Her hands gripped his arm, tighter than before.

Veterinarians will tell you that during the full moon, the animal hospitals see a rise in cat and dog accidents and pet related injuries up to thirty percent. Lions, usually nocturnal animals, will begin to hunt during the day when the moon is full. The more the gravitational pull on an animal, the more insane they will come. Many deny this, but the evidence remains solid. Even if this idea is completely false, it could only give credence to the actions of the cats. He hugged her tightly, staring into the tree.

"Susan." she said.

"W-what?" he managed to say, looking at her briefly, then back up to the tree.

"I never told you my name." she said.

"Nice to have met you Susan. I'm Zane."

It was the last thing that either of them ever said.

Detective Jumpers and The Case of the Missing Wallet

Professor Bimple was a big man. He didn't like plums or the color purple. He had a cat named Frumpy and he taught math at Little Town College.

One day as he was sitting in his orange chair, he heard Frumpy meow.

"Oooh, Frumpy! you must be hungry!" the Professor said. "Let me get you some food."

Professor Bimple went to the cupboard and realized that he was out of cat food. He also saw that he was out of lemons and sandwich bags.

So he went to the grocery store to buy cat food, lemons and sandwich bags. He saw his friend Mrs. Turtledove buying some ice cream. She waved hello as he went to the front to pay. As he reached for his wallet, he realized that it was gone.

"Gone!" he exclaimed. "How could my wallet be gone?"

"Where did it go?" The clerk asked him.

"I have no idea" the professor said. "But I know someone who can find out for me."

Leaving his cat food, lemons and sandwich bags, he left the grocery store in search for Detective Jumpers.

Detective Jumpers was at home busy cleaning his glasses. He thought that everyone who needed glasses should take care of them magnificently. He liked things to be magnificent.

Professor Bimple burst in and shouted: "They've stolen my wallet! Thieves and vandals! You have to do something detective!"

The detective had been very organized in his glasses cleaning. He had taken them all apart and each piece was laid out on the table in a magnificent order. When the professor burst in, the Detective jumpers jumped out of his chair, and the whole table fell over, scattering the little pieces everywhere.

After the commotion had settled, Professor Bimple apologized.

"I am sorry Detective Jumpers; I didn't mean to make you jump! But they have stolen my wallet!"

The good detective looked around and then down at his glasses. Then from a pocket in his shirt, he pulled out another pair of glasses and put them on. You should always have a spare pair of glasses handy, just in case.

"Well then good Professor, we shall have to catch them! Quick! Get my Crime Kit!"

Now the famous Jumpers Crime Kit was magnificently large. Since Detective Jumpers was so thin, he usually had someone else carry it. It was a good thing that Professor Bimple was a big man.

Grabbing up the kit, the two of them returned to the grocery store.

By this time at the grocery store there was a long line. They were all waiting for Professor Bimple to pay for his cat food, lemons and sandwich bags. Everyone sighed a sigh of relief when they saw Detective Jumpers and his Crime Kit.

"Let us review what has happened" said the detective. "First of all... Where were you when you realized that you didn't have your wallet?"

"Why I was right here!" said Professor Bimple.

"Aha!" said the Detective. And he reached into his Crime Kit and brought out a notebook and a pen. He wrote down:

"Grocery Store - No Wallet"

Mrs. Turtledove spoke up just then: "Yes, it's true! I saw him here!" She smiled, but then she noticed that her ice cream was melting and dripping into her shoe. She stopped smiling.

"Professor Bimple", the clerk asked, "Are you going to pay for your cat food, your lemons, and your sandwich bags?"

"Yes!" he exclaimed. "But first the Detective has to find my wallet!"

"Hmmm... Let me think for a bit." Detective Jumpers thought for a bit. Everyone in the grocery store was holding their breath.

"Aha!" Detective Jumpers shouted.

Everyone jumped.

"Did you walk here?" Asked Detective Jumpers.

"Why yes, yes I did!" said Professor Bimple.

"Then Follow me!" Detective Jumpers said.

So Detective Jumpers, carrying his notebook; Professor Bimple, carrying the Jumpers Crime Kit; Mrs. Turtledove, carrying her shoes; and the clerk carrying Mrs. Turtledoves ice cream all left the store.

They walked back to the professor's house.

Frumpy met them at the door. She was still meowing.

"Now tell me professor," the detective said, "what were you doing before you came to the store?"

"I was looking in the kitchen for cat food."

They looked in the kitchen.

Detective Jumpers wrote down:

"Kitchen - No Wallet"

Mrs. Turtledove said: "Where were you before the kitchen?"

Frumpy meowed.

"In my orange chair!" Professor Bimple said, and then he said to Frumpy: "Shhhh Frumpy!"

They all went over to the orange chair and looked in it. No wallet.

Detective Jumpers wrote down:

"Orange Chair - No Wallet"

Then Detective Jumpers noticed something magnificent. A clue. Tiny footprints from the chair going up the stairs.

Detective Jumpers said: "Professor Bimple, do you have midgets living here?"

Everyone thought that was funny. The clerk from the grocery store snorted.

Detective Jumpers wrote down:

"Orange Chair - Footprints!"

Then he reached into the Jumpers Crime Kit and pulled out his magnifying glass. It made things look very large. He examined the prints.

"Why these aren't from midgets at all... These belong to a cat."

Frumpy meowed.

Everyone looked at the her.

"Frumpy! Did you take my wallet?!?" Professor Bimple asked in a loud voice.

She purred, turned and walked away. They all followed her.

She walked down the hall and into the bedroom and went right onto the bed. There, by the bed was Professor Bimple's wallet.

"Why, Frumpy!" Professor Bimple said. "You didn't take my wallet! It was here all along!"

"Another case closed." said Detective Jumpers.

"Well, it looks like we can celebrate by eating the rest of this ice-cream." said Mrs. Turtledove.

Everyone thought that was magnificently funny.

The clerk from the grocery store even snorted again.

Poems

Just because

Just because I love you
and just because you're true

I decided to write a sweet poem
and dedicate it just to you

I've used all the words I can
to tell you how I feel

Hopefully you'll realize
my emotions are for real

You're the love of my life
the sun on my face

These feelings I have
no one can erase

I'll love you my sweetheart
forever and a day

No, not even time or death
can take that love away

Set the pace

My soul is poured out like water,
My spirit tires of me,
I have nothing left but you Lord,

I have nothing left but Thee.
This is my story,
And also my prayer,
That you, dear Lord, will set the pace,
And you will take me there.

Fire Station #666

When the Spirit of truth ignites the kindled flame
Inside of you begins to burn up, up and around again
And you begin to transmit a smoke-signal to show
Where the holy fire burns, for the wind of Yah to blow

The alarm goes out round creation... Fire in the east
Something has combusted! The flame will need to feed
Where the candle under basket: is hidden, dull and safe
The Wildfire of the Spirit... catches, licks, and leaps.

The Nephilim hear alarms and burst into full speed.
And Fire Marshall Lucifer hops on his trusty steed.
Racing to the fire-spout, to extinguish every ounce
The Fire Station #666 is ready on the pounce

But Yah is in control this day, to burn away the dross
And purge the world from its sin, to satisfy the cross
For every rooftop now alights, and angels now rejoice
The Pentecostal backdraft rush, as if creation had a choice.

The glory that has come at last, is power that will stay
Where winds of doctrines come and go, but I they will not sway
For my heart is on fire, and it scorches to the core
The revival cry has come again as I lie as dead upon the floor

The tempest has blown over, The lava cooled to rock
I looked about and saw, gold dust upon my smock
And trembling I did realize the truth revealed aghast

Yahshuah Ha Mashiach, unshaken to the last

We control the transmission

We are the brothers of destiny, and the rulers of thought
We are those inside your mind and your TV
We are the small voices in society
We are the left hand of the rulers
We are the right index finger of dictators
We are the nutritional information on your cereal box
We are the food pyramid
We are the FBI FDC NAACP IRS and the wedding cake
We will tell you what you are
We are the school system
We are the judicial system
We are NBC ABC CBS FOX and the Sunday brunch
We are those whom you forget
We are the new car commercial
We are the system you buck
We are the street evangelists
We are your funerals
We are your gods
We are your tarot cards
We are your hatred
We are the bar you love
We are the one
We control the transmission
We are I am who are you
We are you in disguise

Mirror

She walked to the grave
Wary of bystanders

She walked

Looking down upon him
Wretched and shaking
She looked

Peaceful and quiet
he seemed
breathing relief

Not like I remember
She thought
Not at all

So vibrant and alive
Now cold as stone
Cold and dead

Witness protection
Breast implants
She saw himself


```
              where rabbits sleep deep
```

there is a man standing at the base of a mountain
he shouts to the hill in front of the mountain
he shouts to the tree line that starts at the base of the mountain
he does not shout at the mountain

though the forest creatures see him
they wonder why he does not go up the mountain.
the trees wonder why he does not wander into them
the peak of the mountain calls
the clouds beckon
the sky beckons

and the clouds part and he sees the full mountain
and he falls down at the revelation

so the man at the base of the mountain cries out
so the man at the face of the mountain calls out
he calls to the God of the mountain
he calls out to the sides of the mountain

he calls to the stream that runs out of the mountain
he calls to the mountain
the mountain sees him
and the mountain hears him
yet he does not walk up the mountain

he has some courage
for he recognizes the journey
he has mapped out the trail that leads up the mountain
he is drawing maps to travel up the mountain

he is calling out to the mountain telling it to harken to his maps
he is building vessels to collect spring water
he is fortifying his shoes, his shirt, his tools
and yet the mountain pathways gather pine needles

the mountain does not move
it is before the man
and the man has gathered a crowd
the mountain paths and trails go unwalked

and the mountain is tall
and the mountain is majestic
and the mountain is all that is before them
and the mountain is alone

and the man builds a forestry station
he creates pamphlets about mountain safety
he sells walking sticks and postcards
he has services about mountain life

and other people come to hear him
and they pitch their tents
and they also dress in mountain gear
and they eat campfire food

the campfire life
camping out
mountain life
the winds of the hills
hillside mornings

the children of the mountain people grow
they have built houses
they build their houses so all windows face up the mountain
they have mountain community center services

one day a little girl was playing alone
she looked up the mountain
at the base she noticed the trailhead
and a little rabbit eating a leaf

she left her mountain man playset
and she got up and chased the rabbit
the rabbit ran into the tree line
at the base of the mountain
and she followed it
setting foot on the trail that led up the mountain

where will she go up the mountain
way up the mountain, up into the mountain
she goes to where the rabbit sleeps deep
way up into the mountain
she goes, she goes, she goes

and the campfire calls out her name
and the men walk around the trailhead
and the women mourn around the trailhead

and the mountain knows the girl
and the mountain sees the girl

and the mountain cares
and the mountain shares
for the girl is alone, the girl is cold
and the rabbits have left her in the snow

the girl passes on deep in the snow
and into the mountain she flies
and tries and calls out to the women
at the base of the mountain
with their pamphlets and their trail-mix

she calls to them to come join her
in the mountain up in the mountain
where the rabbit sleeps deep
inside the mountain up in the mountain

they hear not the cries of the girl
they hear not the cries of their girl
they hear the cries of the mountain
the wraiths that live on the mountain

the wraiths are the mountains'
the wraiths are the brave walkers
the walkers of the trails
that those who camp below
can only dream of walking

walking up the mountain
into the snow
where the rabbit sleeps deep

walk with me
walk with me
walk with me
into the snow

she cries
walk with me
into the snow
where the rabbits sleep deep
and the lost dreams grow

Spontaneous song #7

I give one thing
I give you my life
I give you all things
I give you my search for a wife

I give you all things
Cause here I am
Just a man

Summer Sunshine

Play hours all day sun; play, play, play.
In the summer sun, warm and shiny.
Summer sunshine, summer funshine.
Smiles and glistens, warm and friendly.
Shimmer and glimmer, warm and nice.
Hot and funny, play sun, play.
Play on lakes, and play with shade.
Play with ice in lemonade.
Cheery and happy, careless and free.

Warm summer sunshine, come play with me.

For everything...

For every string that is tied down.

Another string is loosed somewhere.

For every man in battle gown.

Someone is broken two in prayer.

For every wrong there is a right.

For every day there is a night.

And every sinner who can't cope.

There is a God, there is a hope.

A Song with Words

This is just a song
Written out in words
Of how I have loved you
How you have always been my first

I was just a boy
Looking only for himself
But now that I've found you
I am wanting something else

I love you
There is no denying that
I love you
And that is a matter of fact
Oh I love you

And you will always be the one
I run to
I want to
To love you

Essays

Burgerman

Burgerman lived in Chicago. He was half blind and half deaf from a grenade explosion in Vietnam. He had never enjoyed reading, and had never found anything on the radio worth listening to... but he enjoyed talking to people, and he enjoyed making people smile, and he enjoyed making hamburgers.

He ran his own vending cart in the downtown Chicago area. He sold the best damn hamburgers anyone had ever had the opportunity to bite into. He put up signs saying so too. He was the busiest vendor on the block and he always made money.

Burgerman had paid his sons college tuition with the money he made from hamburger sales. Like I said, He always made money.

His son was home for the holidays, and was helping his dad out with the business, when they began talking about the economy. "Dad, the economy is in the worst shape it's been in years. And things are only looking worse for the future."

Well, He believed his son. His son had been to college. His son knew things that He didn't know. And maybe it was his imagination, but people had looked grumpier recently. Burgerman took down his signs. He couldn't afford them anyway; and he started using cheaper hamburger. People started to go elsewhere for their hamburgers. Soon there was almost no business at all.

"Son, you are right." Burgerman said, "The economy is in bad shape. Nobody wants to buy Hamburgers anymore."

bones

The technology will point one will win one adding that you do how often wondered long Dixons and men if this testimony to hang in tow beat Duncan give you good kiwi.com to open in normal common+ in the Caribbean and you mentioned Emmy-in the national union-long jump and televisions perfect than in bowl should speeches peaches the Jews shipped sheet in of the winners in the low technology will play one more and will win one in league do well to Milan one gift since and since this new series of speeches Wendell and to the longevity of men have in William we get me for him so fearlessness bulky not affect trouble was did time there's things that never knew and happened happening, it is invalid will bolts or thou are war will this and subject for it and will will present here's my door were arrested this is the oracle for from reason for it in some-but my nose with her to sell the bee's news those who see no reason for the year for four old infant care ward told the lives of the vision worse before they what he is the words the rules will increase its old hospice of you're the worst old "but the bow before even the Colma he sold a lot posterity rules for him in the told of the lord to come to grief" and how at Montclair white Christmas people in the work of the four will give himself "also is in Zaire" their group point for the field for weapons of war see award this one will just them Balkans and her staff workers were: they signed him to flee of the warriors uses by review in the Jay Gould wider than works for cast and what they see the path I will go we're week were or the war will be those of the zone said war from its owner of the outcome is a lot of them to will it work for by time server you buy some first them but still have some tell the goal of improving moved Dow had better and they would not comment of my life is that the law of the "white paint".

The Conjunction of History

I didn't ever want to go through that situation again where I was on stage and everyone knew I was doing horribly. And I knew that I knew nothing about preaching through the written word (and I actually still don't)... However! I was now an official twenty-one year old man, and I had best start figuring things out. Seminary was helping me a little, but if I didn't help myself, then I would never grace the pulpit again, and that was somehow a worse fear.

While I was at Seminary, I had several paying jobs that I used to support myself. The steadiest was at the Seminary itself and the church connecting to it. I was a custodial engineer. I worked third shift, plunging toilets and emptying trash. Not a glorious job, but it helped pay some of the bills. It was late one evening and I was praying to God about what I should do with my life and I stopped because I heard the audible voice of God speak directly into my mind. I was asking over and over: "What should I do with my life? What should I do with my life?" And an answer came back to me: "Preach, Write, Sing."

So, here I was, called to preach. I was called to write. I was called to sing. The rest of my life was glorious and I moved mountains with my "FAITH." Amen.

Except, not really. I had failed at preaching, I had failed at writing... The singing gig was going alright. Everyone loved to hear me, but there wasn't enough work to go around and they wanted me to do it for free. I needed to reach higher, I needed to learn, I needed to understand how to get there... How to accomplish what God had literally spoken to me to do... Buuuuuuut, in order to not die too young by reaching too high (or whatever Icarus did) I would come back to reality and investigate what made me, the me that I was. So I began studying.

I studied the Bible. I was looking for an explanation as to:

A)   Why I had failed so miserably at preaching
B)   Why I had failed so miserably at writing
C)   Who the gosh-golly heck was I anyway?

Although I'm still looking for the first two answers, I was sure I could determine who I was immediately. I had to find that out at least. You know the adage - If we don't remember our past, and learn from it, we are doomed to repeat it. Something like that at least.
So I began the dig.

Pauly Hart:

A)   Who was he?
B)   Where was he from?
C)   How could he accomplish his three purposes in life?

Answer:

My family heritage reaches to the proud purchase of the Transylvania
Colony from the Cherokee by North Carolinian Richard Henderson and
forged by Daniel Boone. It was purchased legally by the Natives but was
shortly done away with by the Self-appointed do-gooders at the Virginia
General Assembly. This caused the lawful and legal contract of the
Cumberland Gap from the Natives to be invalidated and stolen, ceded to the
newly formed "United States" government.

Notwithstanding that I have accrued such a basis from my forefathers, most
of my people moved from the Carolinas to Texas, by way of Indiana. My
great-great uncles, Orville and Wilbur Wright, were some of the
descendants that never left, and played with bicycles and eventually gliders.

My mother and her father, being good Southern Baptists, decided that the
only way to protect the great state of Texas, from the United States as well as
Mexico, was to join the Foreign Mission Board and defend Mexico from
within the borders of Mexico from an even angrier threat, that of Red
Communism... Specifically that of M-26-7 and a certain Fidel Castro and
Minister Khrushchev. Because, obviously, the way to the United States was
through Mexico, and the way to Mexico was through the sacred heart of
Jesus-on-the-cross, and the only way to get there, was through the Bible
translated into Spanish... So let's protect the Spanish Bibles... Obviously.

While my mother grew up in Mexico, learning how to pick cotton and be a
missionary's kid with her two siblings, my father's father was in Somolia,
Africa, reading the seismographic information from the off shore reserves
between Garad and Kismayo - throwing dynamite off of a boat. Free seafood
for everyone. His wife, my grandmother, a good woman of Levitic heritage,
would struggle to raise my father and his two older siblings in Texas.

My parents would meet at Texas Tech, years later. My father stole my mother away from his friend, and tennis double. My father became my mother's Trigonometry tutor and my mother, obviously, become in love. They wed, moved to Indonesia, where I spent my formative years as a child - An alien white-haired blue-eyed boy in a sea of brown.

Concurrently, being a legal Native American European Mexican African American Israelite, it struck me that the conclusions to my research into my heritage had left me with more questions than answers.

The only real conclusions were questions:

Maybe I was born to be awkward.

Maybe I had awkwardness thrust upon me.

How I killed Garnal.com

i was sitting at home reading up on the local job market and i found a really interesting one involving a company car and it seemed great at $16.00 per hour.

i left them a message and forwarded my resume'.

boom.

i got a wonderful letter back from "Mary XXXX" telling me to go to http://garnal.com/ and fill out the application.

ok.

i go there and page one is blah blah blah disclaimer.

page two is a link to a credit score.

page three is the credit score asking me for my address, phone number, email, credit card and social security number.

oh yeah like i'm going to give that out.

so i go to google.com and look up garnal.com.

NOTHING

so i look up the registrar of the domain.

here he is:

Linh XXX XXXX, Admin
XXXX Tower 1, Lippo Centre Hong Kong XXXXXXXX, XX
Telephone #: +XXX-XXXX-XXXX

i called him.

got a voicemail.

i said: "i know where you live, i know what time you get out of bed, take down garnal.com or there will be trouble." in a really rough voice.

three minutes later i went back to it on my PC and couldn't see the website anymore. i now show: "Site is currently maintenance."

poof.

but just to be sure of that, i tried from another IPA and bam. same thing.

so hopefully we never see garnal.com again.

hopefully.

-pauly hart
10:07am
10/29/10

10:10 am update

ok they are running another scam from stonecrestlending.com as well.

they are using a XXXXXXXX/XXXXXdomain hider called domains by proxy inc. to mask their intentions but for now http://www.XXXXXXXXX/XXXX/XXX/XXXXX points to the spam site.

i called richard XXXXXXX at XXX-XXX-XXXX who seems to be the man responsible for XXXXXXX.com but just got the voicemail.

i didn't leave a message.

kinda scary leaving yourself so exposed richard.

i know it's early at lyris technologies in emeryville california, but you shouldn't run scams like this no matter where you are. you and Linh are seemingly bad people.

Books Were My Friends

You know what's fun? Waking up one day and realizing that all of your friends think you're insane. Soon after my baptism, I was moved to a private school. Make no mistake, I was a problem child and was moved around every couple of years. It was easier to do it this way than try to reform the hooligan that was Mister Pauly Hart. At the first private school I went to we had an actual "Religion Class" where we learned all about the fabulous Martin Luther and how he started the Reformation Movement. It was pretty cool. Very structural and methodic but there was still room in my heart for the non-metaphorical Christ. It was just harder to find Him inside of all the organized religion that was presented to me. The Lutherans had a very different viewpoint on the working hand of God than the Baptists or Charismatics.

This doesn't mean I didn't try my hardest to get my questions answered. I would come up with some zingers and they wouldn't have a clue what to do with them. You want to really annoy a dead religious person's ethos, you start asking them about a living and active Creator. Oh boy, watch out. There's no one more defensive than a religious guy who "knows" he's right. And, of course, when I transferred to yet another school, the same thing happened. So I went to 4th-6th at a private Lutheran school and 7-10th (my parents stepped up their game) they sent me to a Mennonite Academy out in the middle of nowhere. Dress code and all that - Yargh. It was even more strict. Still had a "Religion Class" but at least we talked about more than Luther. We also talked about Mennonites! Ooooh. So exciting. Well… It wasn't all bad. Chapel was often fun. But my Religion teacher often sent me to the Principal's office (or the Superintendent if he was really in a bad mood.) Once he told us that if he didn't believe him on a subject, we could look it up in the dictionary! So I got out of my seat and got the dictionary on his desk. Yes, another trip to the Principal's office.

Why you gotta kill the child for a desire to learn? I don't know. The only thing I came away from that school with was some good stories. Religion it seemed, was lost on me. But only at school. Home life, was another matter altogether.

I am an introvert. I don't like crowds, I don't like parties, I don't like mixers, I don't like groups. I don't generally like people. As I am writing this I look to the other laptop beside me where "Alone" Season 3 is queued up ready to play. "If only…" I sigh. Such is the mind of me: A hermit and a weirdo by choice and by blessing. The fact that I live with another introvert as her husband is an irony seldom lost on me. But let me rewind. From a young age all I ever wanted to do was play with Legos and read comics. Reading and building fantasy worlds led me quickly into Role Playing Games where I could be a ninja thief who could steal jewels and slay dragons. The fantasy world was often larger than the real one. My dad would have none of this and thrust me into Boy Scouts to enlarge my mind and rectify my moral compass.

So in Boy Scouts, (guess what Dad) we played Role Playing games and read comics. Anything that had to do with outer space, wizards, Martians and warlocks was within bounds. And I loved every moment of it. Marvel Comics and Palladium Role Playing Games when I was forced to be on the bus ride home or at Boy Scouts, and when I was alone? It was H.G. Wells and DC Comics. Nothing was better than Saturday when I could watch

Transformers, G.I. Joe, Super Friends, Space Ghost and Flash Gordon. And, if I wasn't in the mood for re-runs I would get by with Spider-Man, Hulk and Shazam. But I would relive those fantasy worlds all weekend long and straight into the next week. As long as it didn't have anything to do with reality and relied heavily on deep Science Fiction, I was into it.

www.ingramcontent.com/pod-product-compliance
Lightning Source LLC
Chambersburg PA
CBHW030544200626
46812CB00020BA/1819